On this date

31st October 2008

a **Fairy Godmother**

appeared in the Wonder Window to help

Eden Amelie Sheldrake

(Name)

discover the beauty, love and spirit in

every living creature.

Illustrated by Martha-Elizabeth Ferguson.

ISBN: 0-9634910-8-3
Library of Congress Card Number: 2001088275

10 9 8 7 6 5 4 3 2 1 First Edition March 2002
Printed in China

My Fairy
Godmother

Samara
Anjelae

In memory of

Daisy and Bigfoot

A special thanks to Isabella, a literary cat.

BelleTress Books

While we each have a Guardian Angel, a Fairy
Godmother is a gift given only to those who appreciate
and respect nature and all living creatures – from the
tiniest of insects to the largest of animals. Your Fairy
Godmother can be a Lady of the Woods, a Guardian of
the Sea or a Garden Spirit. To be enchanted with a
Fairy Godmother, we must find a secret gateway to
Fairyland. It is then, and only then, that we can hope
to have a visit from our Fairy Godmother.

The Fairy Gateway lies in every Wonder Window. If you believe in fairies, you will find fairies. Look closely and you will see them. Fairies are the little people who carry the life force that gives nature its color, form and beauty. They are busy helping make the grass greener, the trees stronger, and the flowers more beautiful. Fairies will bring you ideas, make you smile and laugh, and show you the secrets of nature.

Fairies are very talented. They can change their size and appearance at will. Their shapes are often free flowing and hard to describe. These bright beings can have wings like angels or they can look like humans. They can be tiny or of considerable size. It depends on the particular work they have to do. Fairies usually dress in the clothes and follow the customs of the land in which they live.

Those who can see fairies are individuals who are at peace with nature – Mother Nature lovers. People who work with their hands – artists. Souls who are wise – seers. Beings who are kind and giving – humanitarians. And Fairy Helpers – those who are kind to animals.

A Fairy Godmother has Special Powers

Playing Music

Foretelling Events

Making you Sleepy

Bringing Good Luck

Drawing Animals Near

Delivering your Wishes

Appearing and Disappearing

Keeping Secrets and Treasures

Working Magic with the Weather

Before you enter
Fairyland, you must learn
the fairy rules. Do not talk about
fairies in a bad manner or they will leave you and
you may never see them again. Say thank you when a fairy leaves
you a gift such as a feather along your path, a special stone, the beautiful
scent of a flower or a lost item returned. Do not tell anyone about the
presence of a fairy without first asking permission from your fairy friend,
and if it is supposed to be a secret, then keep it a secret.

When you see mushrooms in a circle, be respectful and step around
them. It is a fairy ring. When you spot trees with a hollow hole filled with
branches and twigs, know that it might be a fairy or animal home and
should be left alone. Learn by watching fairies and animals in their natural
habitat, not by capturing them.

Fairy Signs

Sparkles of light around plants and flowers

Items vanishing and appearing again

Sudden unexplained goose bumps

Unidentified music and singing

Bending of grass blades

Sweet scents of flowers

Uncontrolled laughter

Puzzling loss of time

Soft crinkling noises

Rippling of water

Delicate breezes

Fairy rings

FAIRY GODMOTHER ALPHABET

F is for Finding Fairies when no one else does.

A is for Appreciating Animals and the Little People.

I is for Inviting fairies into your life.

R is for Receiving nature's gifts.

Y is for Yielding to fairy requests.

G is for Giving to Mother Nature.

O is for Opening your heart to fairy love.

D is for Deciding to believe in fairies.

M is for Making Magic with the Wee Folk.

O is for Offering your help to animals.

T is for Thinking about the wonders of the world.

H is for Hearing with your Heart rather than with your ears.

E is for Entering Wonder Windows.

R is for Resting assured that you have a

Fairy Godmother

Fairies love to celebrate. On
Fairy Festival Days they come from
the water, air and earth to dance,
sing and enjoy Mother Nature. Fairy
Festival Days include the Autumn and
Spring Equinox. This is when the sun
crosses the equator and day and night are
equal. They also celebrate the Summer and
Winter Solstice when the sun is farthest from
the equator. The equinoxes and solstices mark
the beginning of each season. Other reasons
for celebration include a Shooting Star,
a Morning Moon, a Rising Red
Sun, a Radiant Rainbow and
Your Birthday.

Are you drawn to the water, or would you rather be near a campfire? Do you like to watch the birds in the air, or be out in a garden working with the soil? There are many types of fairies. Turn the page to discover the earth, fire, air and water fairies.

Earth Fairies are also known as gnomes. They like to work with stones and minerals and create jewels. Gnomes live in trees, bushes, grasses and plants. They frequently have long beards, wear red caps on their heads, and dress in materials which they create. They pay little attention to humans because they are busy working and caring for their own families. The best times to see and talk to the earth fairies are when they are resting.

Fire Fairies are known
as salamanders, not to be confused with
the animal known as the salamander. Behind
every fire there is a Fire Fairy that helps make the
flame. They are small, usually between two to twelve
inches. Fire must be controlled and respected if it is
to be of benefit to fairies and to the environment.
They will work hard to build a fire if your
intention is wise, like a campfire where
storytellers bring laughter and
closeness. Fire Fairies like it when
you ask for their help and thank
them for their kindness.

Air Fairies are known
as sylphs. They plant creative ideas in
your mind. These divine beings can be
colorful in their dress, or if they choose,
they can become invisible. Many times a
fairy comes up with an invention and
passes it on to an earth being. When you
are creating art, or just feeling inspired to
create something, pay attention and see
if you have an air fairy helping you.

Water Fairies are
known as undines or water spirits.
You can see them riding the waves of
the ocean, dancing on lakes, resting on
marshy land, or fluttering around
flowers that grow in watery places.
Undines are clothed in a shimmery
substance that resembles floating
chiffon. They usually have wings of gold
and silver. The best time to spot water
fairies is at sunset and sunrise.

Fairy Likes

Daisies

Animals

Rainfall

Gardens

Laughter

Ladybugs

Butterflies

Honeybees

Dragonflies

Lilac Bushes

Storytelling

Kind People

Secret Places

Magic Wands

Sparkly items

Animal lovers

Hidden treasures

Children (little people like themselves)

Fairy Dislikes

Trouble

Loud Bells

Dirty Water

Unclean Air

Forest Fires

Grumpy People

Startling Noises

Harmful Chemicals

Unflattering Fairy Tales

Anyone who disrespects Nature

Messy rooms (except for closets)

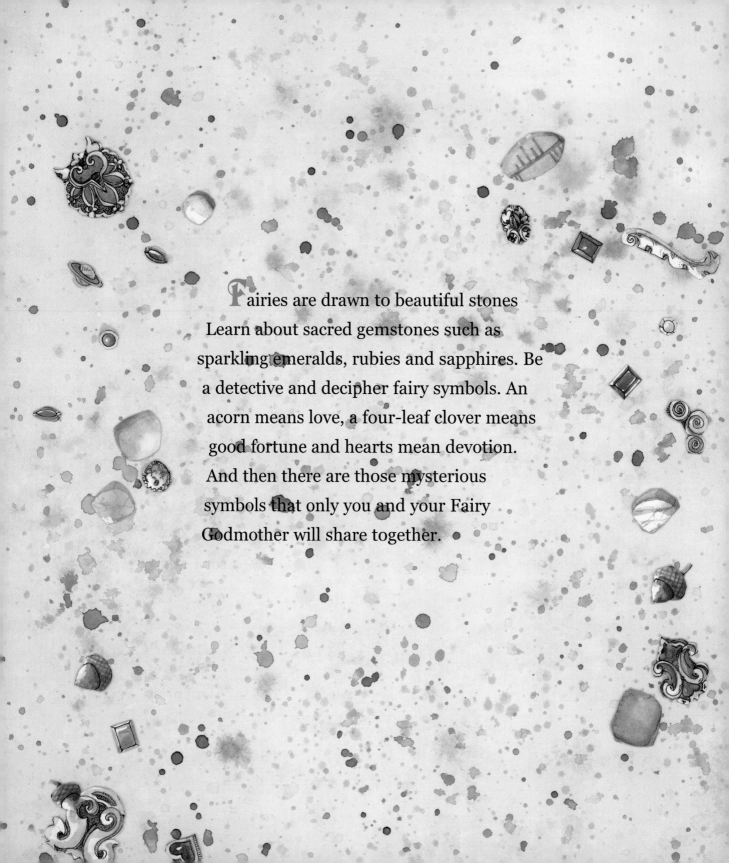

Fairies are drawn to beautiful stones
Learn about sacred gemstones such as
sparkling emeralds, rubies and sapphires. Be
a detective and decipher fairy symbols. An
acorn means love, a four-leaf clover means
good fortune and hearts mean devotion.
And then there are those mysterious
symbols that only you and your Fairy
Godmother will share together.

Make a Fairy Godmother Treasure Chest.
A decorative box or a pretty container will work.
Include notes about your wishes, hopes and
special treasures. Try writing a story or poem
celebrating the beauty of nature. Be outside in the
presence of fairies when you compose your piece. Each
time you add to your chest, know that your Fairy
Godmother will keep your treasures safe and secure.
When you make an effort to express your love for the
earth, you are helping to build a better place for all.
Remember, every tree, rock, flower and animal
has something to teach us.

Fairy Colors

Really Red

Bonkers Blue

Go-Go Green

Purple Passion

Yappy Yellow

Boomerang Black

Glittering Gold

Laughing Lavender

Chilly Chartreuse

Fun Fuschia

Oops Orange

Artful Aubergine

Wild White

Silly Silver

Fairy Delight (rarely seen)

To the eyes, stars do not look like they have much color. Yet, like fairies, they actually range in hue from red to purplish white. Remember stars are only visible at certain times, just like your Fairy Godmother. Search the Fairy Kingdom, especially around flowers, and you will find the gateway to Fairyland.

Fairy scholars recommend the "tween times" and "tween places" for spotting fairies. The "tween times" are those times that are undefinable. Dawn and Dusk – neither day or night. Noon – neither morning or afternoon. Midnight – neither one day or the next. "Tween places" are places in the natural world that are neither one place or another. It is the intersection of two worlds, like lakeshores, where glades grow in the woods, or at fences and border hedges. Extend an invitation to meet the Wee Folk at a "tween time and place."

Fairies are called by many different names.
Sometimes they want their names to reflect their true
identites. Through history, some tales portray fairies as
mischief makers. Some of them are, but for the most
part, they have only good in their hearts. To find fairies,
learn how to address them by their favorite names.

Devas

Gentry

Wee Folk

Little People

Moss People

Tree Shadows

Bright Beings

Nature Spirits

Forgetful Folk

People of Peace

Good Neighbors

Elves

Trolls

Pixies

Sprites

Gnomes

Brownies

Elementals

Leprechauns

Keepers of Memories

Sidhe (people of the hills)

Mother Nature's Children

Be Like a Fairy

Sing Often

Be Colorful

Ride a Horse

Talk to a Tree

Notice Beauty

Rest by Water

Paint a Picture

Listen to Birds

Be a Storyteller

Help an Animal

Be around Flowers

Play an Instrument

Shimmer in the Sun

Take a Nature Walk

Find a Kitten Purring

Make a Dog's Tail Wag

Walk Barefoot in the Grass

And when others say they don't believe in fairies, or in a Fairy Godmother, smile and go on. One day when they live in harmony with nature, they will discover Wonder Windows, where fairies exist and dreams come true.

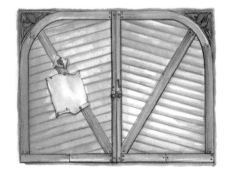

Wonder Window Series

A collection of timeless books that are a treasury of soul wisdom,
making them fine gifts for all ages.

Other books in the Wonder Window Series:

My Guardian Angel, an enchanting
book that promotes a deeper understanding
of angels and our relationship with our
Guardian Angel. A Guardian Angel is
assigned to every soul's Wonder Window for
guidance, love and protection throughout
the journey of life.

My Magical Mermaid, a mesmerizing
book that journeys into the mysteries of the
seas. A Magical Mermaid arrives in the
Wonder Window sharing the gifts of the sea,
the treasures on earth and the magic in life.

BelleTress Books